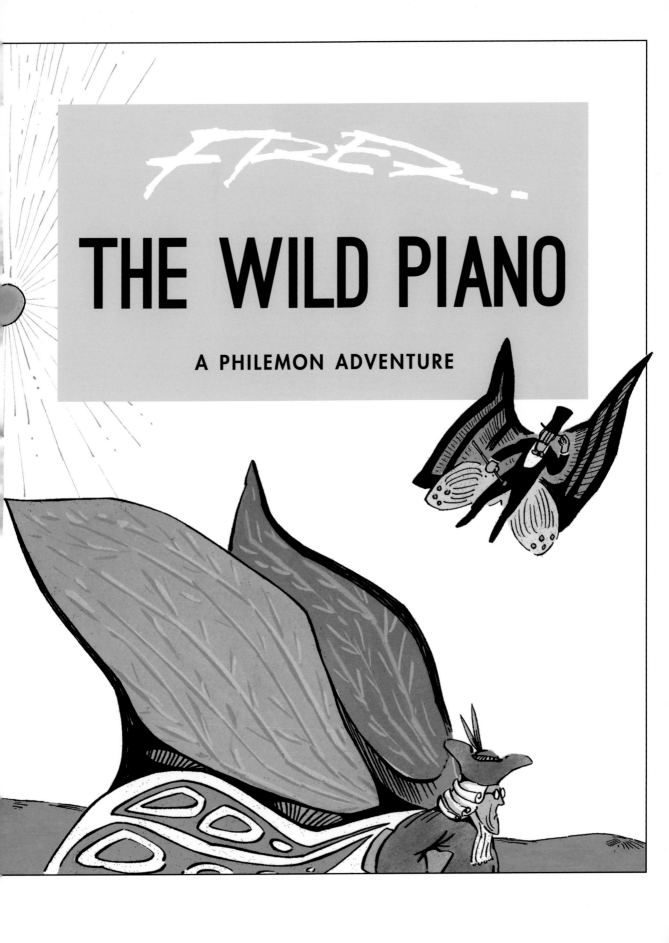

FRED

THE WILD PIANO

A PHILEMON ADVENTURE

Editorial Director & Book Design: FRANÇOISE MOULY · Translation: RICHARD KUTNER

Hand-lettering: MYKEN BOMBERGER & FRED · FRED'S artwork was drawn in India ink, watercolor, and gouache.

ABDOPUBLISHING.COM

Reinforced library bound edition published in 2017 by Spotlight, a division of ABDO, PO Box 398166, Minneapolis, Minnesota 55439. Spotlight produces high-quality reinforced library bound editions for schools and libraries. Published by agreement with TOON Books.

Printed in the United States of America, North Mankato, Minnesota.
042016
092016

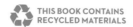

THIS BOOK CONTAINS RECYCLED MATERIALS

FOR VISUAL READERS

TOON GRAPHICS

WWW.TOON-BOOKS.COM

LIBRARY OF CONGRESS CATALOGING-IN-PUBLICATION DATA

This book was previously cataloged with the following information:

Fred, 1931- author, illustrator. [Philémon et le piano sauvage. English]
 The wild piano : a Philemon adventure / by Fred; translated by Richard Kutner.
  pages cm. -- (The Philemon Adventures)
Originally published in French by Dargaud in 1973 under title: Philémon et le piano sauvage.
Summary: "Determined to save his friend the well digger from the labyrinth on the second 'A,' Philemon returns to the parallel world of islands that form the words 'Atlantic Ocean.' He finds himself on the 'N' where he inadvertently breaks the law, goes on trial, and is sentenced to confront the wild piano"-- Provided by publisher.
ISBN 978-1-935179-83-2
1. Graphic novels. [1. Graphic novels. 2. Adventure and adventurers--Fiction. 3. Islands--Fiction. 4. Alphabet--Fiction.] I. Kutner, Richard, translator. II. Title.
PZ7.7.F73Wi 2015
741.5'944--dc23
          2014028860

ISBN 978-1-61479-503-2 (reinforced library bound edition)

ABDO
Spotlight
A Division of ABDO
abdopublishing.com

THE WILD PIANO

A PHILEMON ADVENTURE

A TOON GRAPHIC BY

FRED.

MEET PHILEMON

PHILEMON IS AN IMAGINATIVE TEENAGER WHO LIVES ON A FARM IN FRANCE, BACK IN THE 1960S. WHEN A MESSAGE IN A BOTTLE SPARKS HIS CURIOSITY, HE FALLS RIGHT INTO A WORLD OF FANTASTIC ADVENTURES...

ANATOLE IS A DONKEY, PHIL'S TRUSTY FRIEND. HE TRIES TO HELP HIM STAY OUT OF TROUBLE, BUT PHILEMON'S ADVENTUROUS SPIRIT AND CURIOSITY GET THE BEST OF HIM.

HECTOR IS PHILEMON'S GROUCHY FATHER, WHO REFUSES TO BELIEVE PHIL'S WILD STORIES.

AFTER HE FALLS DOWN THE WELL, PHILEMON WAKES UP ON A STRANGE ISLAND IN THE MIDDLE OF THE ATLANTIC OCEAN, WHERE HE MEETS **MR. BARTHOLOMEW.**

...THEN YOU'RE THE WELL DIGGER IN THE LEGEND?!

THE LEGEND? WHAT LEGEND?

WELL, IN MY VILLAGE, THEY TELL THE STORY OF A WELL DIGGER WHO NEVER CAME BACK UP FROM THE WELL HE WAS DIGGING FORTY YEARS AGO.

TOGETHER, PHIL AND MR. BARTHOLOMEW TRY TO FIND A WAY BACK, BUT THEY LOSE EACH OTHER IN A LABYRINTH.

BLAH, BLAH BLAH. BLAH BLAH!... BLAH BLAH BLAH BLAH BLAH BLAH BLAH BLAH BLAH...

PHILEMON!

IT'S JUST UNBELIEVABLE!

I'VE BEEN TALKING TO YOU FOR FIVE MINUTES, AND YOU'RE NOT EVEN LISTENING TO ME. ARE YOU DREAMING?

SORRY, DAD! I WAS THINKING ABOUT BARTHOLOMEW.

BARTHOLOMEW?

YES, THE WELL DIGGER.

GULP

MUNCH YUM

HE'S STILL A PRISONER IN THE LABYRINTH... AT THE BOTTOM OF THE WELL...*

HMPH...

*SEE: CAST AWAY ON THE LETTER A

I'VE HAD IT WITH YOUR STORIES!

BUT, DAD, THEY'RE NOT STORIES. AT THE BOTTOM OF THE WELL THERE'S...

HOWDY, EVERYONE!

UNCLE FELIX!

HMPH!

HEE HEE HEE HEE!

PUFF PUFF

YOU'RE JUST IN TIME, FELIX!... TRY TO REASON WITH PHIL. HE CAN'T STOP TELLING ABSURD STORIES.

YEP! THAT'S TEENAGERS FOR YOU!...

CLOCK CLOCK

HEY, MIND YOUR MANNERS!

WHEW! WALKING AROUND IN THIS HEAT MADE ME THIRSTY. HEE HEE!

PUFF

HAVE A SEAT!

SO, PHILEMON, WHAT KIND OF STORIES HAVE YOU BEEN TELLING?

WELL, I WAS TELLING DAD ABOUT BARTHOLOMEW...

THE WELL DIGGER?

YOU KNEW HIM?

OF COURSE! HE WAS A FRIEND OF MINE, GOOD OLD BARTHOLOMEW. MY BEST FRIEND, MAYBE...

HMPH!

WE DID A LOT OF THINGS TOGETHER. YEP, THAT'S FOR SURE. HA HA HA! TRIPS AND ALL KINDS OF STUFF... HEE HEE!

GULP!

THAT'S STRANGE. HE NEVER SPOKE ABOUT YOU.

PURR PURR

PSCHRRRTTT...

WHAT? YOU... YOU SAW BARTHOLOMEW?

WHERE? WHERE DID YOU SEE HIM?

WELL... ON THE "A" OF COURSE...

NO, PHIL, STOP! DON'T EVER MENTION THAT LETTER HERE!

TELL ME, PHILEMON... WHO SPOKE TO YOU ABOUT... UH... ABOUT THE...

ABOUT THE "A"?

SHHHHH... NOT SO LOUD, PHIL, NOT SO LOUD...

HMPH!

BUT I WENT THERE, UNCLE FELIX. THAT'S WHERE I MET BARTHOLOMEW. FRIDAY WAS THERE, TOO... HE'S A CENTAUR...

YES, I KNOW HIM...

HOW IS IT POSSIBLE? AFTER ALL THESE YEARS? BARTHOLOMEW ALIVE... AND STILL DOWN THERE... ALL THE WAY DOWN THERE?

TAP TAP TAP

WHAT NOW?!

ENOUGH! A CASTAWAY AT THE BOTTOM OF A WELL IN A LAND THAT DOESN'T EXIST? COME ON!

I CAN UNDERSTAND PHIL MAKING UP TALL TALES--HE'S STILL A KID. BUT YOU?! TELLING SUCH RIDICULOUS STORIES AT YOUR AGE!

I'M OUT OF HERE. OH, BROTHER! IT'S UNBELIEVABLE...

HUH?

WHY DIDN'T BARTHOLOMEW COME BACK UP WITH YOU, PHILEMON?

ARRRGGGH!

WE GOT SEPARATED IN THE LABYRINTH...

THE LABYRINTH, EH?

PUFF PUFF

THE LABYRINTH OF THE SECOND "A"... YES, IT MAKES SENSE...

PUFF PUFF

BUT HOW DO YOU KNOW?

I KNOW LOTS OF THINGS, MY BOY, LOTS OF THINGS...

I'M SOMETHING OF A MAGICIAN, YOU KNOW...

BUT... IS THERE SOME WAY WE CAN SAVE BARTHOLOMEW?

MAYBE... MAYBE...

WE CAN ALWAYS TRY. BUT...

BUT?

AROUND AND AROUND — THEY'RE MAKING ME DIZZY!

YOU'D HAVE TO GO BACK DOWN THERE.

LET'S GO!

WHERE ARE YOU OFF TO?

TO THE WELL, OF COURSE.

NO! IT'S TOO DANGEROUS. THERE'S **ANOTHER** WAY TO GO DOWN THERE.

BY WAY OF THE GLOBE.

THE GLOBE?

SHHH!

A SHORT WHILE LATER...

I HAVE WHAT WE NEED AT HOME.

COME IN AND HAVE A SEAT. I'M GOING TO GET THE GLOBE...

HUH?

...AND THE SPYGLASS.

BUT... IT'S A GLOBE OF THE EARTH!

NATURALLY.

BARTHOLOMEW IS HERE, ON THE SECOND "A" OF THE ATLANTIC OCEAN.

IF YOU WANT TO JOIN HIM, IT'S EASIER TO GO BY WAY OF THE GLOBE...

EASIER...

BUT OF COURSE. YOU'LL SEE. FIRST I'M GOING TO MAKE YOU SMALLER WITH THE SPYGLASS... USING ITS LITTLE END.

POOF!

HELP!

CALM DOWN, CALM DOWN! YOU WANT TO SAVE BARTHOLOMEW, DON'T YOU?

DON'T MOVE! I'M GOING TO MAKE YOU EVEN SMALLER...

15

23

FLAP!

FLAP!
FLAP!

FLAP!

SILENCE!

BUT WHAT DOES
ALL THIS MEAN?

SHHH!

I'M YOUR LAWYER.
LET ME TAKE CARE
OF THIS.

?

BUT AT LEAST LET ME
EXPLAIN!

NOT A
WORD! YOU
MUSTN'T
SPEAK IN THE
PRESENCE OF A
LAWYER!

QUIET!

ALL RISE!

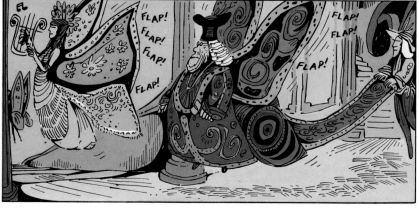

FLAP!
FLAP!
FLAP!

FLAP!

FLAP!
FLAP!

FLAP!

24

Before the PHILEMON trial begins, we find it necessary to recount the history of the ban on bouncing on the lawn.

A very long time ago, the Grand Judge WZCHTZKPL AMPPTKPKL THE THIRD issued a decree forbidding the inhabitants of "**N**" from walking on the lawn. Since the entire island is covered with an immense lawn, the citizens were constantly breaking the law.

Above: the Grand Judge, victim of his own decree.

Those who were able to escape the guards made an effort to raise themselves above the lawn. From generation to generation, these efforts transformed the inhabitants — wings gradually began to appear on their backs, and it is thus that they began to fly. Thereafter, the decree was naturally changed into a ban on bouncing on the lawn.

Let's end this digression and continue with the trial.

THE ZEBRA JAILS ARE THE ONLY ONES ALLOWED TO WALK ON THE LAWN.

AND I AM THE KEEPER OF THE ZEBRA JAILS.

YOU WILL BE LOCKED UP IN YOUR ZEBRA UNTIL THE DAY OF THE **GREAT CONCERT.**

FLAP!
FLAP!
FLAP!
FLAP!

?

GREAT CONCERT?

YES! WHEN YOU COMBAT THE **WILD PIANO**, IN OTHER WORDS.

GOOD-BYE! DON'T TRY TO ESCAPE. NO ONE HAS EVER SUCCEEDED IN ESCAPING FROM A ZEBRA JAIL.

STOP MOVING, YOUNG MAN. YOU'RE TICKLING ME!

FLAP! FLAP!

FLAP!

WHAT WOULD ANATOLE SAY IF HE COULD SEE ME NOW?

Inside the Zebra jail, the days pass, always the same...

But one morning...

OKAY, WAKE UP! TODAY IS THE BIG DAY!

?

FLAP FLAP FLAP FLAP FLAP FLAP FLAP FLAP FLAP FLAP

BUT—WHERE ARE WE GOING?

TO THE CONCERT.

TODAY: BIG CONCERT ON THE WILD PIANO!

TICKET PRICES

?

BONG!

AH! HERE'S THE PRISONER.

HURRY UP! IF ALTERATIONS ARE NEEDED, YOU'RE GOING TO BE LATE.

THAT SHOULD BE THE RIGHT SIZE. TRY IT ON.

HMMMMM... WONDERFUL! IT FITS LIKE A GLOVE.

HMM!

30

ZZZZ
ZZ
ZZZ

HMM...

THERE'S SOMEONE HERE...

ZZZ
ZZ
Z ZZ
Z...

ZZZ... MMMAMGHMM MMHMM... WHAT'S GOING ON?

MR. BARTHOLOMEW?!

PHILEMON?! WHAT ARE YOU DOING HERE?

WHAT ABOUT YOU?

OH MY, DON'T EVEN TALK ABOUT IT.

WHERE'S MY HAT?

I'VE WANDERED IN THE LABYRINTH FOR DAYS... AND I STILL AM WANDERING... FROM HALLWAY TO HALLWAY... FROM ROOM TO ROOM... OH MY...

OH, HERE IT IS!

IT'S A NICE HAT...

YOU MEAN THIS ROOM IS PART OF THE LABYRINTH? THE LABYRINTH OF THE SECOND "A"?

YEP...

SO... THE "N" CONNECTS TO THE SECOND "A"... HMMM... BY AN UNDERWATER TUNNEL... IT'S POSSIBLE... WE MUST BE IN BETWEEN THE TWO LETTERS.

?

FOLLOW ME! WE HAVE TO FIND THE WAY TO THE SECOND "A." I KNOW THE WAY OUT ONCE WE GET THERE.

YES, MAYBE...

THE WAY OUT... OH MY, OH MY... I'D HAVE BEEN BETTER OFF STAYING ON MY ISLAND, WITH ALL THE COMFORTS OF HOME, MY MAN FRIDAY, AND ALL THE REST...

BRRROOM

QUICK! IT'S GOING TO CRUSH US!

THE C-C-C-C-C-CARPET!

QUICK! OPEN A DOOR!

CRUSHED BY A CARPET! THAT TAKES THE CAKE!

HURRY! QUICKLY!

YIKES!

WHAT? SOMEONE DARES TO INTERRUPT THE REVOLUTIONARY TRIBUNAL?

CUTE HAT!

TO THE GUILLOTINE!

LIVE FREE OR DIE

CLOSE THE DOOR!

WHAT DOES HE MEAN, "CUTE HAT"?

UM... EXCUSE US, IT'S...

PHEW! THE CARPET IS GONE...

OUT!

THERE ARE STRANGE THINGS HAPPENING BEHIND THESE DOORS...

Down the well, in a world of utter fantasy...

Frédéric Othon Aristidès (1931-2013), known as Fred, was one of France's most influential and revered cartoonists. Born in Paris to a Greek immigrant family, Fred encountered the myths and stories of many different countries. His mother first exposed him to British literature and, as he grew older, he started to read Edgar Allan Poe, Charles Dickens, and Oscar Wilde. In the sixties, Fred co-founded *Hara-Kiri*, the leading satirical publication of the May '68 movement–he designed its first 60 covers. Philémon, his story for young readers, was first published in *Pilote* in 1965 by René Goscinny, the author of the Astérix series. Philémon is Fred's most celebrated creation: millions of young French people have grown up with it, and it has inspired many of today's most talented cartoonists. The Philémon stories are densely populated with allusions to various literary and artistic sources, all woven together with Fred's unique absurdist logic. While there's no knowing where exactly he found this inspiration, Fred said he often got his best ideas while taking a bath.

Alice in Wonderland

Sir John Tenniel, "Giant Alice watching Rabbit run away," 1865.

Lewis Carroll's influential fantasy novel *Alice's Adventures in Wonderland* was first published in 1865. In it, a young girl named Alice follows a rabbit down a rabbit hole, where she undergoes transformations and has many strange adventures with odd characters. *Alice in Wonderland*, as it is often called, plays with logic and turns it on its head. Alice takes part in the trial of the Knave of Hearts, which proceeds chaotically, with the Queen of Hearts asserting that the sentence should come before the verdict. The same lack of logic and inversion of reality are seen in Philemon's trial. His lawyer, who was not present at the supposed crime, is a witness against him, and there is a hostile, tyrannical judge, who blames Philemon when he smashes his own finger with his gavel.

In this
Style
10/6

Arenas

The Ancient Greeks often attended plays in outdoor theaters, or amphitheaters (from *amphi*, meaning "around" and *theatron*, meaning "place for viewing"). The Romans adapted the Greek amphitheater into the "arena," which was used for a variety of forms of entertainment, including gladiatorial combats. The word arena comes from the Latin word *harena*, meaning "sand" or "sandy place," because sand was strewn on the floor to soak up the blood. These arenas, in turn, led to bullrings, where men (and a few women) fought against bulls, doing all kinds of fancy moves, just like Philemon with the wild piano. If you look carefully, you can see that the wild piano has hooves like a bull. Many bullfights in Spain and southern France still take place in Roman amphitheaters. Modern-day sporting events, like football, take place in a kind of arena, also called a stadium.

Gulliver's Travels

The giant prisoner who has been waiting years for his croissants could be a reference to Lemuel Gulliver, the main character of *Gulliver's Travels*, by Jonathan Swift, published in 1726. Gulliver, like Philemon, loves

to travel. He finds himself prisoner to a race of tiny people in the island country of Lilliput. This is just the start of Gulliver's amazing adventures, however, which include time in the land of Brobdingnag, where people are twelve times as tall as humans, and a visit to the flying island of Laputa.

Arthur Rackham, "Lilliput," 1904, *Gulliver's Travels*.

James Gillray, "The heroic Charlotte la Cordé," 1793.

An early cartoon of the trial of Charlotte Corday, who killed revolutionary leader Jean-Paul Marat.

Georg Heinrich Sieveking, "The Execution of Louis XVI," 1793. *Engraving.*

The Revolutionary Tribunals

The French Revolution of 1789, in which the royal family was overthrown, was followed by a period of political violence and mass executions now known as the Reign of Terror. The Revolutionary Tribunal was first set up in 1792 for the trial of "enemies of the revolution," those who voiced their disagreement with the new ruling party. Prisoners could not have lawyers defend them or have witnesses speak on their behalf. Death was the only penalty, and there was no appeal. In less than three years, thousands were brought to trial and sent to the guillotine, a wooden machine set up in a public square. A large, heavy blade dropped down to chop off the head of the offender.

The Lion, the Witch and the Wardrobe

Philemon and Bartholomew get back home by coming through a wardrobe, an homage to the C. S. Lewis classic *The Lion, the Witch and the Wardrobe* (1950), the first of seven books of the Chronicles of Narnia. In Lewis's fantasy world, four children enter a wardrobe and find themselves in Narnia, a fantastic land of talking animals and mythical creatures ruled over by the White Witch. The children must save Narnia and their own lives, just as Philemon must save himself from the wild piano.

Winged Creatures

Winged people and creatures appear in stories and myths from around the world. In this book, humans grow butterfly wings. In world mythology, wings are usually a sign of magic, and resemble the wings of birds or butterflies.

Sixteenth Century, *Codex Telleriano-Remensis.*

Huitzilopochtli, the Aztec god of war and the sun, is represented with hummingbird wings or feathers.

Guido Reni, "Archangel Michael." ca. 1636.

Angels are traditionally depicted with human form and feathered wings.

Sophie G. Anderson, "Take the fair..." ca. 1880.

Fairies are often portrayed with butterfly wings.

Euphronios, 515 BCE, *Eurphonios Krater.* Photo by Jaime Ardiles-Arce, licensed under Creative Commons.

Thanatos, the winged Greek spirit of death. and his twin brother, Hypnos, the spirit of sleep, carry the dead to the underworld. Hermes, the god of transitions and the messenger between the mortal and divine, depicted in the center, has small wings on his ankles.

Tips for Parents, Teachers, and Librarians:
TOON GRAPHICS FOR VISUAL READERS

TOON Graphics are comics and visual narratives that bring the text to life in a way that captures young readers' imaginations and makes them want to read on—and read more. When the authors are also artists, they can convey their creative vision with pictures as well as words. They can enhance the overarching theme and present important details that are absorbed by the reader along with the text. Young readers also develop their aesthetic sense when they experience the relationship of text to picture in all its communicative power.

Reading TOON Graphics is a pleasure for all. Beginners and seasoned readers alike will sharpen both their literal and inferential reading skills.

Let the pictures tell the story

The very economy of comic books necessitates the use of a reader's imaginative powers. In comics, the images often imply rather than tell outright. Readers must learn to make connections between events to complete the narrative, helping them build their ability to visualize and to make "mental maps."

A comic book also gives readers a great deal of visual context that can be used to investigate the thinking behind the characters' choices.

Pay attention to the artist's choices

Look carefully at the artwork: it offers a subtext that at first is sensed only on a subliminal level by the reader and encourages rereading. It creates a sense of continuity for the action, and it can tell you about the art, architecture, and clothing of a specific time period. It may present the atmosphere, landscape, and flora and fauna of another time or of another part of the world. TOON Graphics can also present

multiple points of view and simultaneous events in a manner not permitted by linear written narration. Facial expressions and body language reveal subtle aspects of characters' personalities beyond what can be expressed by words.

Read and reread!

Readers can compare comic book artists' styles and evaluate how different authors get their point across in different ways. In investigating the author's choices, a young reader begins to gain a sense of how all literary and art forms can be used to convey the author's central ideas.

The world of TOON Graphics and of comic book art is rich and varied. Making meaning out of reading with the aid of visuals may be the best way to become a lifelong reader, one who knows how to read for pleasure and for information—a reader who *loves* to read.

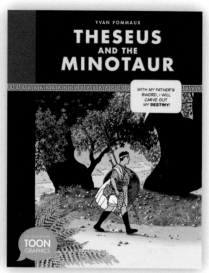